TOM'S REMEMBRANCE

BY REBECCA O'HANLON NUNN

A Heritage Book

The Westphalia Press

ILLUSTRATED BY RICHARD T. HAYNES

Library of Congress Cataloging in Publication Data

Nunn, Rebecca O'Hanlon
    Tom's Remembrance.
    (A Heritage Book)
    Summary: A five-year-old boy meets his grandpa in heaven and begins to find out what life after death is all about, and receives a gift of growing remembrance from his best friend on earth.

    [1. Life in heaven - Fiction. 2. Trees - Fiction. 3. Relatives - Fiction.] I. Haynes, Richard T., ill. II. Title.
ISBN 0-915637-06-5

The Westphalia Press
The Dohman-Boessen House
Loose Creek, Missouri 65054

Printed in Japan
First printing, December 1987
                10 9 8 7 6 5 4 3 2 1

This book was set in Goudy Old Style and composed by Show-Me Typographers, Jefferson City, Missouri.

Editor: Bill Nunn
Art direction: Richard T. Haynes
Design: The Nunn Group
Production: Bill Nunn

For the love
of all children
and their parents

In memory of Tom Wekenborg

Please, Lord,
could you hold him
if he's scared?
And could you tuck him in?
He doesn't have his bear.

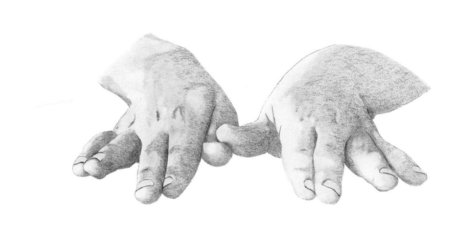

FOREWORD

Rebecca Nunn's story for little children about heaven and life after death is a moving story about a little five-year-old boy, who meets his grandpa in heaven, and tries to know what life after death is all about. It will touch the hearts of many children and grownups, who read it to them. It will give them an idea about the reality of life after death, where we are reunited with loved ones, and where we learn to adjust to a different level of existence, surrounded by love, understanding and compassion, where we can be in touch with those we leave behind on the planet earth, and where we continue to grow and look forward to further growth, which continues for, in our time language, eternity.

This storybook will be a great contribution to the ever-increasing literature for children, to make them aware that although death may come prematurely to our little ones, that is is not the end of our existence, that it's a transformation into a richer life with continued growth, and an increasing awareness of unconditional love.

Thank you, Rebecca, for writing this story, and for helping children and their parents to shed their fears of death and to understand that those who have loved and contributed something to this physical planet will have a wonderful time when they make the transition we call death.

Elisabeth Kubler-Ross, M.D.

T om peeked over his Grandpa's shoulder. He saw the brown-and-white checkered bear Grandpa was sewing together for him and he couldn't help giggling.

"That bad, is it?" asked Grandpa without looking up from the bear.

Tom made his face quit smiling. He wouldn't hurt his Grandpa's feelings for anything. "No sir. It's nice...and different."

They both studied the bear a moment in silence. Then Grandpa's laugh broke the stillness. "He is different at that, Tom."

Tom's new bear was made out of the checkered brown-and-white shirt that Mr. Abner had come to heaven in. And the bear's ears were made from Mrs. Sterner's hat. Her hat was red felt, which made pretty funny-looking bear's ears.

But it was the tail that had made Tom laugh. The tail was a snipped-off piece of Grandpa's gray beard. It looked so funny sitting on the end of the bear's seat. The wisp of beard reminded Tom of the inside of a bird's nest he'd seen once that had fallen out of the willow tree next to the back porch at home. Tom had wanted to put that nest back, but he hadn't known where to put it.

"Why did those stupid birds build their nest in a willow tree?"

"What's that?" asked Grandpa.

Tom didn't realize he'd spoken out loud. "Just thinking, Grandpa," he said softly.

"Ahhh, yes." Grandpa nodded and was quiet while Tom closed his eyes and thought of the willow tree in his back yard. The minute he did — there it was! And there was a big fat robin in it. Maybe it was his nest he'd found that time.

Tom smiled and opened his eyes. This was a neat trick! One of the things he liked best about heaven was the "thinking and it's here". Grandpa taught Tom this when he first came. It worked for everything. People, too.

He just thought of his Mom and Dad and there they were! You didn't even have to close your eyes. Tom did because that was what he used to do when he made a wish. Except this was a lot better than just plain wishing! On earth, he'd never gotten his wish right away before. Sometimes he'd never gotten it at all.

Tom laughed. "It's like magic!"

"It is...isn't it!" Grandpa agreed.

"I'm glad you were here in heaven to come to meet me, Grandpa." Tom patted his Grandpa's shoulder.

"I'm glad, too, Tom."

"Did someone come to meet you, too?"

"Yes. My mother, remember?"

Tom remembered then. Grandpa's mother had the sweet smile and the braids on top of her head. And Grandpa's father had the loud snort for a laugh. They were nice. They loved him, too. Just like Grandpa loved him..even though Grandpa had died before Tom was born. That reminded Tom of a question he wanted to ask.

"Grandpa? How did I know you when you came to meet me?" Tom remembered he wasn't scared at all. There was this bright light. And then the most beautiful music he'd ever heard. Better than any on radio and T.V. And his Grandpa had said: "Over here, Tom." And there Grandpa was in the light! He was smiling big and his arms were open wide.

Tom had run to him immediately.

"Oh, you know lots of things after you're born to heaven, Tom."

Born to heaven. Tom smiled, He liked that. Back on earth—people used to say someone died. It always sounded bad, that word. Died. But here you said Born to heaven. That was another thing Tom liked about being here. And he liked picnics with no ants and mosquitoes and wasps...falling down and not getting hurt..not having to clean up anything because nothing ever got messy...catching a ride on sailclouds...flying like a bird with all that good swooping and diving stuff...swimming in Grandpa's lake—and he hadn't even known how to swim before! And fishing in Grandpa's lake, too.

There was only one thing he didn't like about being in heaven, but he tried not to think about it. He hadn't even told Grandpa. If he did, it would make Grandpa feel bad. And he didn't want to do that.

Besides, nobody ever felt bad in heaven. Well...mostly nobody. Maybe it was just because he was new. Maybe that's why he couldn't stop thinking about his remembrance.

Grandpa looked up from the bear, and saw Tom staring at it. Grandpa didn't know that Tom wasn't even thinking about the bear because he was thinking about something else. He pulled Tom to him on his lap.

"I'll bet you think it's kind of silly, huh. Me sewing this bear?"

"Oh, no, Grandpa!" Tom hugged his neck tight.

"Even when you can have a hundred bears just by 'thinking and it's here'? And when you already have your own bear?"

"Mama always liked what I made her better than the money-bought stuff."

Grandpa grinned big. His smile looked like an upside down rainbow—all bright and happy. "Yes, yes! That's exactly it, Tom. I didn't ever get to make you anything. I like making things. And somehow if I "think and it's here" for stuff to make your bear out of, it feels like cheating."

Tom nodded. "I'm going to like having my very own bear you made, Grandpa. And so will Teddy!"

Tom used to take Teddy with him when he stayed all night with Grandma Brummelwitz. Teddy—and his blanket, too, when he was a real little kid. Grandma always said, "Now let Tom bring his blanket." even when he was too big to bring it, "It'll make my house seem more like home."

"Does God want me to feel at home, like Grandma did?" Tom asked suddenly.

"You bet your boots He does!"

"And that's why we have 'think and it's here'?"

"Right. And that's why we come to heaven in our own clothes. And He lets us keep them until we don't need them anymore."

"You think God would take my cowboy boots?" Tom hated to think about giving up his boots. His Dad had given them to Tom on his last birthday.

"Of course not! Not if you want them," Grandpa said.

"Will I wear a housecoat like yours when I don't need my jeans and shirt anymore?"

"Housecoat?" Grandpa looked down at his flowing cloud-like garments. "You know I think you're right, Tom. This outfit does look like a housecoat. From now on I'll call my robe my 'heavenly housecoat?' "

Grandpa let out a war-whoop laugh then. Tom laughed as hard as Grandpa. Grandma used to tell Tom, "Why, when your Grandfather laughed, I swear the rafters in the barn shook!"

That reminded Tom of something else. "Grandpa, tell me again about your remembrance." Even though he wondered about his own remembrance, it was still Tom's favorite story. And it was Grandpa's favorite story, too. He always grinned awhile before he told it.

Tom settled back against Grandpa's chest and waited.

"Well, Tom, my remembrance on earth is my barn. I built it from the floor up. Did a dandy job, too! Now I had neighbors help me, but I have to tell the truth. I did most of it myself."

"And when people looked at it, what did they say?" Tom asked eagerly, even though he knew the answer.

Grandpa cleared his throat. And his voice sounded rich and deep, like a good yell down a drainpipe. "People see my barn and say, 'Old Jake Brummelwitz was quite a man! Look at that barn, would you? Solid as a three-hundred-year-old oak, that barn!' "

TOM'S REMEMBRANCE

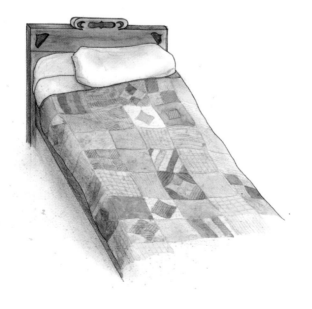

Grandpa and Tom sat together and thought about Grandpa's remembrance.

Finally, Tom said, "And Mrs. Sterner's remembrances are her quilts?"

"That's right, Tom. Each of her daughters and sons has a quilt made by her."

"Grandpa?"

Grandpa didn't answer. Tom turned around and saw him staring at the lopsided, checkered bear. Grandpa's whole face was a frown. He shook his head. "I maybe built a good barn, but I'm sure making a mess of your bear. Would you look at this?"

"Grandpa?" Tom said louder.

"Mmmmmmm? What is it, Tom?"

"Uh...I forgot." He'd been tempted to ask Grandpa if he could help Tom figure out how he could get a remembrance. But if he couldn't—then he'd feel bad for Tom. And he'd been working so hard on that bear, and having trouble with it. Grandpa was what Tom's mother called a "softie."

Tom wished he could stop thinking about a remembrance. But he couldn't. His Grandpa and Mrs. Sterner stayed back on earth long enough to make a remembrance. And he hadn't. This was the one thing about being in heaven that bothered him.

He was worried his friends would forget him because he hadn't made a remembrance.

TOM'S REMEMBRANCE

He was just five years old and he hadn't known about remembrances. Grandpa had told him the first time he told Tom about his barn that remembrances weren't necessary at all. He said it was just something mostly old people had because they'd been on earth so long they'd had to do something while they were there.

He'd said that everyone who loved Tom would remember him—that's for sure! Tom knew his Mom and Dad and Grandma Brummelwitz, and Grandma and Grandpa Turner would remember him. But what about his friends?

None of them would ever look at anything and say, "Look at that! That's old Tom's. Isn't that something?"

Tom sure wished he'd known about remembrances when he'd been on earth. What would he have made? he wondered. A house? No. That would have been too hard. How about a doghouse? Too hard, too. What could a five-year-old kid make for a remembrance, anyway?

TOM'S REMEMBRANCE

"I think I'll ask Mrs. Sterner if she can do something for this bear," Grandpa said.

Tom got up off Grandpa's lap. He knew he should tell Grandpa that the bear looked just fine. But Tom felt too sad to try and talk right now.

"She's probably in her garden— or over by my lake. I swear she likes my lake better than her garden. I kidded her the other day, saying she's going to have to get one of her own if she starts fishing in it!

"Want to come along, Tom?"

"No, thanks, Grandpa. I'll play around here awhile. Or go find Eddie."

Grandpa nodded and headed toward his lake. Tom had been surprised when he was born to heaven to find lots of earth things here. But, then, he hadn't known about "think and it's here" yet.

He sure wished it worked for earth, too. 'Cause if it did...he could do a "think and it's there" instead of a "think and it's here."

He'd like a small barn there, maybe. Or maybe a birdhouse. If he'd had a little help, he might have made a birdhouse.

Tom sighed and stuck his hand in his jean's pockets. They were empty. That was no good. He needed that black rock of his—and maybe that speckled toad that lived in Grandma Brummelwitz's fruit cellar.

Tom closed his eyes, getting ready to...

"Tom?" A low, gentle voice called his name.
"Yes?"
"Over here, Tom. Open your eyes."

Tom did and a beautiful light shone all around. But he still couldn't see anything.

"I know you're not quite happy here yet, Tom."

Tom nodded. The soft understanding voice made tears come to his eyes.

"And I know why. It's because you don't have a remembrance, isn't it? Like your Grandpa and Mrs. Sterner?"

Tom squinted his eyes quickly, but even when the tears pushed out he couldn't see anything but the light.

"I'm going to show you something, Tom. Close your eyes— like you do for 'think and it's here'— and tell me what you see."

Tom was puzzled, but he did what the nice voice told him. And when he did close his eyes, he saw his best school friend, Jamie, digging in the dirt!

"What do you see?" asked the gentle voice.

"I see my friend Jamie!" Tom said.

"What's Jamie doing?"

Tom kept his eyes closed tight. "He's digging."

"And...?"

"And he's...he's planting a tree."

"What kind of tree, Tom?"

"It's a pine tree. My favorite kind."

"Do you know what Jamie calls the tree?" asked the voice.

"A pine?" Tom was too polite to tell the voice that Jamie knew what a pine looked like. They'd gone to a nursery once on a school bus, and the man there had told them some of the tree's names. He and Jamie both liked the pine tree best.

"No, Tom. Jamie calls it Tom's tree."

"Tom's tree?" Tom whispered. He watched ever so closely now as Jamie patted the dirt around the tree. Then Jamie got up and stood back to look at it.

"Yes, Tom. I know you've been worried about a remembrance. So Jamie, your best friend, is giving you a remembrance. When your tree gets big enough, Jamie is going to carve TOM on it.

"Your other friends will come to see it. And when your tree grows tall and strong, they will say, 'Would you look at Tom's tree? My isn't it fine! And wasn't Tom a fine boy and a fine friend!'"

Tom kept his eyes closed so the voice wouldn't see that he was crying. But he was crying happy. He was so glad to have a remembrance! Just like Grandpa and Mrs. Sterner! He could hardly wait to tell Grandpa. Why, with his remembrance pine that Jamie was planting, and with his other friends coming to see it...he didn't ever have to worry again that they would forget him!

Jamie sure picked a good pine tree, too. Tom smiled. Jamie might even build a secret lookout in it...or find a bird's nest...like I found under the willow tree...and he...oh. He hadn't thanked the voice.

"Sir?"

"Yes, Tom?"

"Thank you. I'm going to like it here just fine from now on. I was worried...just some worried...not real bad...but I couldn't tell my Grandpa because he's a softie."

"And that was very thoughtful. You're a fine boy, Tom."

Tom felt love like a warm hug all around him. He looked straight at the light. "Thank you, sir. I mean God. I didn't know you at first, God."

"Quite all right, Tom. We have plenty of time to get to know each other better now. You'd better run along. I think your Grandpa is calling you. I'll bet he finally finished your bear...with a little help from Mrs. Sterner." God chuckled and the light disappeared as quickly as it had come.

Tom turned and ran toward Grandpa's lake. He could hardly wait to tell him that he had talked to God! And that he had a remembrance now, too!

Tom's tree! And all his friends would see it! Jamie would water it and care for it, just like the man at the nursery had told them.

Tom and heaven were going to get along great now. God sure was nice!

Tom was almost to the lake before he noticed what had happened to him. He had shed his earth clothes, and he had a heavenly housecoat, just like Grandpa's! Gosh it felt good. Kind of light...like air.

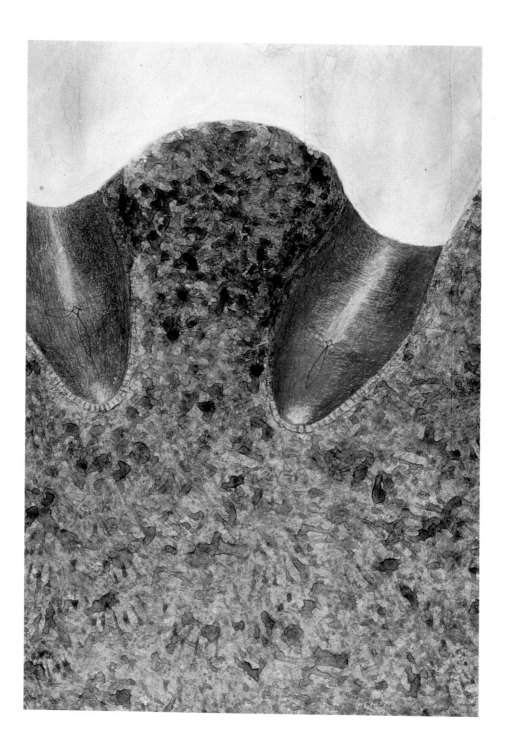

Suddenly, Tom's heart pounded, and he looked down at his feet. Ahhhhh. The toes of his cowboy boots stuck out from under his new outfit.

He smiled. God was smart, too. He knew all five-year-old boys born to heaven needed cowboy boots.

THE END

A Heritage Book

HERITAGE BOOKS are contemporary
works about ways of life worth preserving
in Heaven and on earth.